D0429320

MR. PIG
and
SONNY TOO

by Lillian Hoban

An I CAN READ Book

HARPER & ROW, PUBLISHERS
New York, Hagerstown, San Francisco, London

Mr. Pig and Sonny Too

1403

First Edition

Library of Congress Cataloging in Publication Data
Hoban, Lillian.
        Mr. Pig and Sonny too.

        (An I can read book)
        SUMMARY: Four short stories relate Sonny Pig and
his father's adventures skating, exercising, finding
greens for supper, and going to a wedding.
        [1. Short stories.   2. Fathers and sons—Fiction]
I. Title.
PZ7.H635Mi3   [E]   76-58731
ISBN 0-06-022340-5
ISBN 0-06-022341-3 lib. bdg.

To P., B., E.,
and J. H. too

Ice-Skating

Mr. Pig was sitting

by the fire.

"I am very glad it is

today," he said.

"Why are you glad it is today?"

asked his son, Sonny Pig.

"Because if it is today,

it can't be tomorrow.

Tomorrow is Miss Selma Pig's

Gala Costume Ice-Skating Party,

and I can't skate."

"It is easy to skate," said Sonny.

"Put on your skates

and I will show you."

Mr. Pig put on

his ice skates.

He put on

his earmuffs,

his scarf,

and his mittens.

Then Mr. Pig went outside.

The wind lifted up his earmuffs,

and whipped his scarf

around his head.

"I don't think I want to learn,"

said Mr. Pig.

"It is too cold and windy.

I would rather sit by the fire."

"Skating is fun," said Sonny.

"It makes you warm and rosy."

"All right," said Mr. Pig.

"Show me."

"First you slide on one skate," said Sonny.

"Then you slide on the other.

Now slide on both together,"

yelled Sonny.

Mr. Pig slid on both skates,

but they did not stay together.

One skate slid out on one side of

Mr. Pig. The other skate slid out

on the other side.

And Mr. Pig sat down

very hard in

the middle!

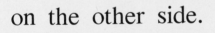

"I don't like skating,"

grumbled Mr. Pig.

"It hurts my back."

"I will tie a pillow on you,"

said Sonny,

"so it won't hurt when you fall."

Sonny tied a pillow on Mr. Pig.

And Mr. Pig tried skating again.

This time, Mr. Pig's skates

crossed each other.

Mr. Pig fell face-down in a puddle.

"Now I am all wet in front,"

said Mr. Pig,

"and I am cold as well.

The wind is nipping my nose,

and I am going to sneeze.

I wish I were home by the fire."

"I will get a blanket for you,"
said Sonny.

"Then you will be nice and warm."

Sonny pinned a blanket on Mr. Pig,

and Mr. Pig tried skating again.

He went slipping and sliding

and gliding on the ice.

"This is fun!" called Mr. Pig.

Suddenly, the wind lifted the

blanket high above his head.

Mr. Pig went flying over the ice.

The wind twisted his scarf

round and round him.

It lifted up his earmuffs.

Mr. Pig flew faster and faster.

"Help!" yelled Mr. Pig. "Stop me!"

Just then, he sneezed,

and fell in a heap.

"Mr. Pig," called Miss Selma,

who was walking near the pond,

"are you practicing for my party?"

"AH-KA-CHOO!" sneezed Mr. Pig.

"What a lovely costume,"

said Miss Selma. "Whatever

made you dress up as a bed?"

"AH-KA-CHOO!" sneezed Mr. Pig.

"I'm afraid he's caught cold,"

said Miss Selma to Sonny.

"We must get him in by the fire."

Mr. Pig spent all that day

and the next sneezing.

He could not go to

Miss Selma's Gala Costume

Ice-Skating Party.

But he won first prize

for the best costume anyway.

"I am very glad tomorrow is today,"

Mr. Pig said to Sonny

as they ate the chocolate cake

he had won.

And he warmed his toes

cozily at the fire.

Exercise

One morning, Mr. Pig

looked at himself in the mirror.

"My clothes have shrunk!" he said.

"Everything is too small."

Sonny Pig looked at Mr. Pig.

"Your clothes didn't get smaller,"

said Sonny. "You got larger."

"You are right," said Mr. Pig.

"I must lose weight.

I will exercise every day

till my clothes fit again."

"Swimming is good exercise,"

said Sonny. "So is hiking."

"Let's pack a picnic lunch,"

said Mr. Pig,

"and we will go

swimming and hiking."

Mr. Pig packed a picnic lunch,

and Sonny packed their

bathing suits.

They put on their hiking boots,

and started to hike.

They hiked over big hills

and little hills.

They hiked across fields

and through woods.

After a while,

Mr. Pig stopped and wiped his brow.

"I think we have hiked enough,"

he said. "Now let's try swimming."

"It is still a long way

to the beach," said Sonny.

"We must keep hiking."

They hiked some more.

Soon Mr. Pig huffed and puffed.

"Let's stop and rest," said Mr. Pig.

"My boots are pinching my toes."

"If we stop and rest,
we will be late for lunch,"
said Sonny.

"If we eat lunch now,
we won't be
late for it,"
said Mr. Pig.

"You are right," said Sonny.

So they found a shady spot

by the side of a stream

and ate their lunch.

"Now," said Mr. Pig,

"I am going to cool my toes

in the water."

He sat on the end of a log.

"Look out!" yelled Sonny.

Mr. Pig landed *kerplash!*

in the water.

"Good," said Mr. Pig.

"We can swim right here,

and still be home in time for tea."

"But you have all your
clothes on," said Sonny.
"Never mind," said Mr. Pig.
"The sun will dry them off
as we walk home."
But as the sun dried
Mr. Pig's clothes,
they shrunk and shrunk
and shrunk some more.

When Mr. Pig and Sonny got home,

Mr. Pig was bulging out of

his trousers.

His shirt was so tight

that his ears turned pink.

Mr. Pig said, "This won't do.

All of that exercise

has made me much larger."

Sonny looked at Mr. Pig.

"You didn't get larger," said

Sonny. "Your clothes got smaller."

"You are right," said Mr. Pig.

"I must give up exercising

or my clothes will get so small

I will have nothing to wear."

And they both sat down

to cream puffs and donuts

and fudge pie for tea.

A Special Pig

Mr. Pig scrubbed behind his ears.

He trimmed his nails

and cleaned his teeth.

Then he brushed his hair carefully.

"Where are we going?"

asked Sonny Pig.

"We are not going anywhere,"

said Mr. Pig.

"Miss Selma is coming to supper,
and I want to look clean and tidy."
"What's for supper?" asked Sonny.

"Oh, a little of this

and a little of that,"

said Mr. Pig. "Nothing fancy."

"Miss Selma always makes

a special treat

when we go to her house,"

said Sonny.

"I know," said Mr. Pig.

"And it will be a special treat
when she comes here.
It is not every day
she sees me looking
clean and tidy."
"Still," said Sonny,
"it is nice to *cook*
a special treat."

"You are right," said Mr. Pig.

"What shall we make?"

"Dandelion greens and

garden cress," said Sonny.

They took a basket and went

to the bottom of the meadow.

A little brook ran wild and free,

and the mayflies darted quickly

in the tall grass.

"It is very wet here,"

said Mr. Pig.

"My feet are quite muddy."

"Sit on that patch of sand,"
said Sonny. "Then you won't
have to stand in the mud."

But the patch of sand

was an ant-hill,

and the angry ants

crawled up Mr. Pig's legs

and bit his bottom.

"OW YOW!" cried Mr. Pig.

He rolled round and round

in the grass.

"Oh dear.

What will Miss Selma think?"

said Mr. Pig.

"My feet are muddy.

My bottom is all ant bites.

My hair is full of grass.

And we still

have not gathered

the garden cress."

"I will gather the garden cress,"
said Sonny. "You can gather
dandelion greens."
Mr. Pig went
to the top of the meadow.
Dandelion greens grew all around,
and the bees buzzed quietly
in a field of daisies.

Mr. Pig pulled a dandelion green,

but it would not come up.

Mr. Pig dug into the earth,

but it still would not come up.

After a while, he stopped.

"Drat it," he said.

"I really look an awful pig."

"My feet are muddy.

My bottom is all ant bites.

My hair is full of grass.

And now my nails are broken, too.

Sonny," he called.

"I must go clean up.

What will Miss Selma think of me?"

"Wait one minute," said Sonny,

"and I will come with you."

"All right," said Mr. Pig.

"I will pick some daisies

for Miss Selma while I wait."

Mr. Pig picked daisies

till Sonny came.

"These daisies are certainly
very strange," said Mr. Pig.
"They make an angry buzzing sound."
"Run, run!" yelled Sonny.

"It's not the daisies buzzing.

It's the bees!"

Mr. Pig and Sonny ran

all the way home.

When they got there,

Miss Selma was waiting.

"Oh, Miss Selma," said Mr. Pig,

"what must you think of me?

I did want to be clean and tidy

as a very special treat."

Miss Selma looked at Mr. Pig.

His feet were muddy.

His bottom was all ant bites.

His hair was full of grass.

His hands were dirty.

His nails were broken.

And he had a very red nose

where he had been stung by a bee!

"I will tell you what I think,"

said Miss Selma.

"I think you are

a very special pig."

And she kissed Mr. Pig

on the tip of his ear,

which was the only place

that was still clean and tidy.

The Wedding

Sonny Pig was sitting in the car.

He had on a new velvet jacket,

and he looked very handsome.

"Hurry up!" he called to Mr. Pig.

"We will be late for the wedding."

"I *am* hurrying," said Mr. Pig.

"First, I must bring these bushes

into the house."

"But we just planted them,"
said Sonny. "They looked so nice
in front of our door."

"Exactly!" said Mr. Pig.
"Someone may take them
while we are out. You can't be
too careful these days."
"You can't dig up bushes now,"
said Sonny. "You will
make a mess of your clothes."

"No I won't," said Mr. Pig.

"I have taken them off."

"Oh dear," said Sonny.

"I know we will be very late."

"Never mind," said Mr. Pig.

"I am sure

they will not start

without us."

Sonny sat in the car

some more.

After a while,

he called to Mr. Pig.

There was no answer.

Then he heard a loud thump

and a good deal

of splashing and groaning.

"Where are you?" called Sonny.

"I am sitting at the bottom

of the shower,"

moaned Mr. Pig.

"I slipped on the soap."

"Are you hurt?"

asked Sonny.

"You will have to go

without me," groaned Mr. Pig.

"I hurt my funny bone."

"I can't go without you,"

said Sonny.

"Now put on your clothes."

Sonny went back to the car.

After a while, Mr. Pig came out.

He was wearing striped trousers,

a velvet jacket, and a

large kerchief around his jaw.

"Now what is the matter?"

asked Sonny.

"Toothache," Mr. Pig mumbled.

"Must get to a dentist."

"If we don't get to the wedding,

everyone will leave," said Sonny.

"Really?"

asked Mr. Pig quickly.

"Your tooth seems

better suddenly,"

said Sonny.

"Let's go."

Mr. Pig got in the car.

They chugged down the road

and up a hill.

The car went slower and slower.

Then it stopped.

"The car is stuck," said Mr. Pig.

"We can't go to the wedding."

"I'll push the car," said Sonny.

Sonny pushed and pushed.

But the car would not go.

"It's very hard pushing uphill,"

said Sonny.

"I know what is wrong,"

said Mr. Pig.

"This hill is going the wrong way.

We should push the car

down, not up!"

"We can't get to the wedding
that way," said Sonny.
"I know it," said Mr. Pig.
Sonny looked at him. "I know
what is wrong," he said.
Sonny got some gas
and put it in the car.
"There," said Sonny.
"*That's* what was wrong.
Now we can go to the wedding."
"Do we have to?" Mr. Pig asked.
"Yes," said Sonny. "We have to."
"All right," said Mr. Pig.

It was a lovely wedding.

"What a good wife

Miss Selma will be,"

everyone said.

"She never got angry,

though Mr. Pig was late

to his own wedding!

What a lucky pig he is."

And Mr. Pig thought so, too.